LIDIJA ŠIMKUTĖ

for dear Koichi,
with warmth and
gratitude,
Lidija Šimkutė
Sept. 2018

SPACES *of* SILENCE

沈黙の空白

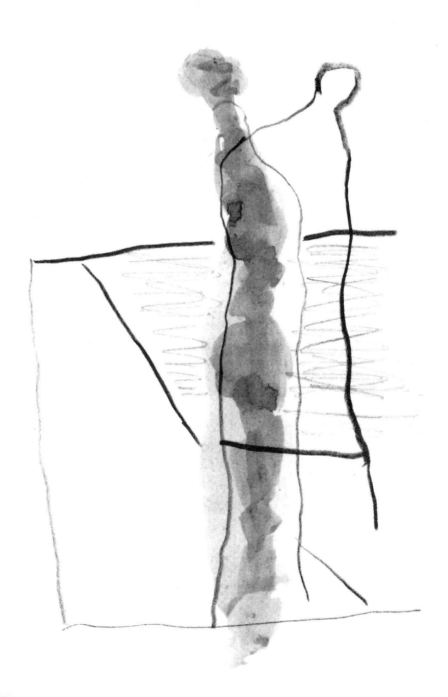

LIDIJA ŠIMKUTĖ

TYLOS ERDVĖS

SPACES *of* SILENCE

Eilėraščiai lietuvių ir anglų kalba

Poems in Lithuanian and English

Poems in English and Japanese

LIETUVOS
RAŠYTOJŲ
SĄJUNGOS
LEIDYKLA

VILNIUS 1999

KNYGOS IŠLEIDIMĄ RĖMĖ

AUSTRALIJOS LIETUVIŲ FONDAS

PUBLICATION SUPPORT

FROM THE AUSTRALIAN LITHUANIAN

FOUNDATION

Iliustracijos / Illustrated by

Viačeslavas Jevdokimovas-Karmalita

UDK 888.2 (94)-1

Ši 69

ISBN-9986-39-108-3

© Lidija Šimkutė, 1999

© Iliustracijos, Viačeslavas Jevdokimovas-Karmalita, 1999

Printed in Lithuania

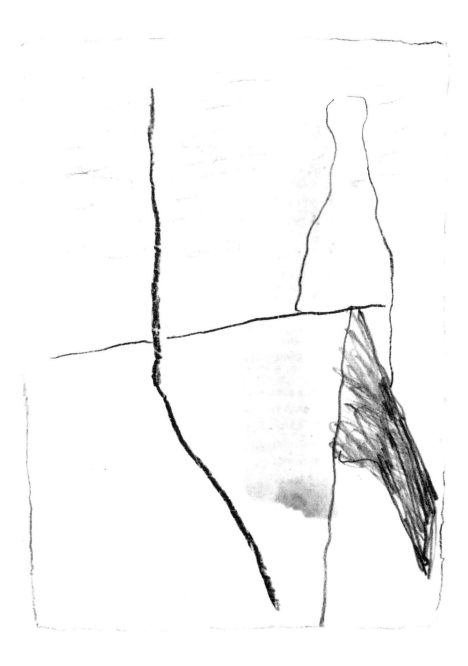

Translator's Preface

Kōichi Yakushigawa

I have translated four books of poems written by Ms. Lidija Šimkutė and then this is a fifth book of poems translated by me. All of them published in an English-Japanese bilingual style.

The deep and sharp shock which I was given on my first reading of her poems has been softened now but her poems are ever charming and challenging. So the readers should always be ready to respond to her challenge and never expect her to tell or teach what she would express.

Now, I would like to read a poem rather than write something general about her poetry.

WATCHING
the distance

*I burn
the colour of Autumn*

Reading this poem, you will be at a loss thinking what the distance is. Usually distance refers to the distance between one and the other. But I think when we read her poems we should discard the binomial way of thinking. The distance which she writes is just the distance and

訳者序文

薬師川　虹一

　私がリジアさんの詩集を翻訳し始めてからこれで五冊目となる。初めて彼女の詩を読んだ時のショックは薄れてきた。しかしリジアさんの詩は何時も魅力的だ。挑戦的でもある。彼女は決して守勢に回らない。彼女は何時も攻撃的である。彼女の鋭い打撃は何時どこから飛んでくるか判らない。読者は常に八方に気を配っていなければならないのだ。カードの奇術師が、思いがけない処から突然カードを出してくるように、彼女の文字は突然思いがけない処から読者の心臓の奥に光を刺し込んでくる。

　それは文字の意味ではない、彼女は文字を意味を伝えるための道具とはしていないし、道具だとは思ってもいないだろう。言葉と文字と意味とが彼女の中では一つになっている。これは当たり前のことのようでありながら、そのとおりにはならないものだ。ラングとパロールの違いという言語学とかの問題ではなく、言葉を物として、言い換えれば、陶芸家の粘土、画家の絵の具、のように言葉、あるいは、文字、を使って彼女の世界を作り上げているのではないだろうか。

　今までも書いてきたことだが、彼女は何かの思想を語ろうとしているのではない、彼女の想いを説明しようとしているのでもない。言葉、文字、はそれ自体彼女の想念であり、読者はただそれだけを追い求めていけばいいはずなのだ。例えば：

　その隔たりを
　　　　見詰め

　私は
　秋色に燃える

nothing more, nothing less. Just the distance. The reader should share the sense of "the distance" with the poet. Then the last two lines will be easy to accept.

Another trial;

WATCH THE SIGNS

that pass unnoticed

in the lavender sky

of sleep

where unexpected

shifts

quicksilver

This is more difficult to follow than WATCHING. Now we should be careful to her use of word. She uses "watch" but not "see". We see something with our naked eye. We take what the eye sees is something real. On the other hand Lidija rejects being under the despotism of the Eye. She is always watching by her own inner eyes or senses within.

という作品を読んでみよう。「隔たり」といえば普通何かと何かとの隔たりを想うのだが、ここではそういう隔たりを想う必要はない。「隔たり」はただひたすら「隔たり」でしかないのだ。それ以上でも以下でもない。「隔たり」という想念が思い描ければいい、というより、「隔たり」という想念を共有できればいいと思う。そうすれば最後の二行を詩人と共に共有することは簡単になるだろう。

　英語の先生風に言えば、I burn を「私は燃える」と訳すか、「私は燃やす」と訳すかの違い、「秋色」を目的語と受けるか、補語と受け取るかの違いなのだが、私には、この詩の世界を二項対立の形とは受け取れないのだ。それは理屈ではない。べつだん詩人が恋人との関係を想い浮かべていると思っても構わないのだが、そんな平凡な世界をリジアさんが描いている、想っているとは到底思えない。

「隔たり」はあくまでも「隔たり」のままであり、決して何かとの間の距離ではないと私は受け取った。その何とも言えない「隔たり」感、それだけの話であって、リジアさんはその「隔たり」感を表現しようとしたのだと言える。私の想いを読者に押し付けるつもりはないのだけど、訳詩はどうしても翻訳者の想いが沁み込んでしまう。そこが翻訳者の辛い処と言えるだろう。

　更に難解な世界がある。

　　徴を見詰めよ

　　ラベンダー色した

　　空の眠りの中で

　　　　フッと

To be free from the despotism of the eye is one secret for reading her poems.

The other secret is to discard the binomial or two-dimensional way of thinking. The sign is not a symbol nor signal. It has something religious sense. But now in this case, Japanese readers, I think, can neglect this. Here the sign is just a sign. We cannot see it nor look at it. It has no fixed form. It has no actual form. It is not a visual thing. Therefore she sings "Watch signs".

I said we should discard a formalism of binomial way of thinking. But Lidija may give us a hint to participate in her secret world. The hint may be found in the last three lines. We should notice the subtle similitude and dissimilitude of "sign" and "quicksilver". Then we can participate in her secret world.

I am afraid if I have written useless or harmful words. I hope the readers to find his/her own way of reading Lidija's poems. If possible try to translate the poems into Japanese, then I am sure, you will have very much exciting experience.

Aug. 18. 2019

消えていく

　　　　水銀の

　　　予想外の変貌

　元の英詩を見てほしい。前半はなんとなくわかる。「徴」とは何だろう、などと考えるのは野暮というものだ。そんな人のために言っておこう、「気配」と言い変えてもいいんだよ。だけど「それではいけないと私は思う。やはりここは「徴」で無ければ。では何の徴かとなるがそれもまた野暮天だ。くれぐれも言っておくが、これは決して「象徴」なんていう無粋な言葉ではないんです。

　後半でそれは水銀の融通無碍(むげ)な姿に置き換えられるが、where以下の英語は、英語の先生泣かせの英語だなあ。それはそれとして、「徴」と「水銀」とのなんという予想外の繋がりだろう。しかしリジアさんはここで少しだけ手品の種を明かしてくれていると、僕は思った。「徴」も「水銀」もどちらも定まった象は無いのだ。それでも二つを組み合わせることによって、なんとなくリジアさんの想いが判ってくるように思えるから不思議である。だからこの二つの繋がりは決して予想外の繋がりではない。そこではリジアさんの鋭い感性が触媒となっているのだ。

　これから私の翻訳を通してリジアさんの詩を読んでくださる読者に余計な先入観を与えることにならないかと心配しながら、ついつい余計なことを書いてしまった。もしなにかを感じて頂ければ、ぜひともご自身で、リジアさんの詩を翻訳してみてください。とてもスリリングな時間を過ごすことができること請け合いです。

　　　　　　　　　　　　　　　　　　令和元年八月十八日

Lidija Šimkutė works as much with space and silence as with words; her poems are full of interestices through which light shines and in which our breath is held as we wait for the next word, the next object, the next bearer of a message, to break through and claim our attention.

The poems larger than their extreme brevity and their few carefully placed words might suggest. The spaces are open views on inwardness.

Silence is that necessary state of attention of waiting, of remaining passive, till the universe, as it speaks through a single object, declares once again it is there.

Difficult as the meanings are that these poems mean and catch since they are always working at the edge of what cannot be expressed, the words themselves when they come have a shining simplicity and precision.
The pictures they call up belong to experience that is near at hand.

This is a voice, a vision, among many, that brings us news of how various the world is and, different as we may be, how much of it we share.

DAVID MALOUF

リジア・シュムクーテは言葉だけではなく、沈黙の空間と取り組んでいる。彼女の詩には様々な事象がみちており、それらを通して光が乱舞し、その中で読者は息を潜め次の言葉、次の対象を待ちうけ、彼女のメッセージを携えてくる次の使者を見てどっと湧きかえり、目を見張るのだ。

彼女の詩は見た目のその極端な短さよりはるかに巨大であり、極めて注意深く配置された僅かな言葉は広大な世界を描いている。空白は内なる世界の開かれた光景なのだ。

沈黙は衝撃を待ちうけるために必要な身構えの状態なのだ。やがて宇宙がたった一つの事象を通して語る時、沈黙は再びその存在を宣言する。

彼女の詩が意味し、捉えようとするものは常に表現可能な世界の瀬戸際で生きているものだから当然捉え難いが、それぞれの言葉が現れる時、言葉はそれ自体輝くばかりの単純・明快さを持っている。彼女の言葉が描きだす世界は身じかな経験世界に属するものなのだ。

彼女の詩は多様な世界の中の一つの声であり、幻想である。それはこの世がなんと多様なことか、しかも我々が互いに異なっていながらその相違を共有していることを改めて知らせてくれるものなのだ。

デヴィッド・マルゥフ

David Malouf
1934年3月20日オーストラリア・ブリスベンに生まれる。オーストラリアを代表する作家・詩人・劇作家。ノイシュタット国際文学賞受賞。

Words are windows, doors half open into space

EDMOND JABÈS

I watched the silence, touched its warmth

CHRISTIAN LOIDL

言葉は窓、ドアは外の世界へ半開き

エドモン・ジャベス

私は沈黙を見詰め、その温かさに触れた

クリスチャン・ロイデル

Edmond Jabès
詩人。1912年4月16日エジプト・カイロに生まれる。1991年1月2日パリで没。

Christian Loidl
オーストリアの詩人 (1957-2001)。イカロスのような生涯だったと言われている。彼の言葉に、「凝視するに値するものは、凝視し得ないものだ」というのがある。

SILK OF THE SPIDER

蜘蛛の糸

INSIDE THE WEB
    of making

we meet and find ourselves
named
    shore
        wind
            river bend

we carve our epics
into driftwood

tread gently
on the waters of no return

紡がれるクモの巣
　　　　の裏側で

私達は出会い私達自身を見つけ
名乗り合った
　　　川岸
　　　　　　巻風
　　　　　　　　曲り川

私達は互いの物語を
流れ木に刻みこみ

戻ることの無い水面を
穏やかに歩む

UNLESS WE DREAM
of each other

there will be no mirror
to shine

the image we seek

もしお互いの
　　　夢を見なければ

私達が求め合う姿を
映す

　　　鏡も要らないだろう

YOUR VOICE
    caught me in flight

I alighted in your palm
    for keeping

あなたの声が
　　　　飛んでいる私を捉えた

私は貴方の掌にとまり
　　　羽を休める

MY BIRD

scratches a letter

    on your window

while morning showers

    sunlight

on white walls

私の小鳥が

あなたの窓に

　　　手紙を刻む

すると朝が

　　　白い壁に

朝日を浴びせる

YOU MOVE
towards me in silence

the language of body
dissolves

seasons of longing

あなたは動く
黙したまま私の方へ

身体が言葉となって
　　　求め続けた

季節を溶かす

I'M AFRAID
> *to take your hand*

> *the lines of my palms*
> > *nurture secrets*

私は怖い
　　　あなたの手を採るのが

私の掌の錯綜する線は
　　　秘かな想いを育てている

ACROSS DISTANCES

I trace your form

web the silk of the spider

to the hum of earth
the crashing sky

I stir the salt in air
tread sharpened rock

melt into sand

遠く離れていても
私は貴方の姿をなぞれる

クモの絹糸で紡ぐのは

大地の呻き
蒼穹の悲鳴

塩からい大気をかき乱し
鋭く尖った岩を踏み

　　　砂の中に溶け込む

THE SNAKE RETURNS
with its eyes in the grass

the river waiting

we have to be silent
as snake eyes of the water

蛇は戻ってくる
眼を叢に潜ませて

　　川は待ち構える

水のような蛇の目となって
言葉を出してはならない

BY THE WINDOW
    lilacs
whisper of cicadas

a gesture of hand
    opens
      the fern flower

窓の傍で
　　　　ライラックは
蝉の囁き

掌のひと振りで
　　　　シダの
　　　花が開く

ON WINGS OF BREATH

I lull you to sleep

all my vertebrae are singing
your name

in the names
of rivers and flames

寝息の羽に乗って

　　　私は貴方を眠りに誘う

私の椎骨の全てがあなたの
名前を唱えている

川と炎の
　　　名にかけて

THE SEA IN OUR EYES

海は二人の目の中に

THE CITY'S EYES
change colour and form

washed sky
dresses bare roofs

the day swallows the dream
among the bones of the wish

都会の目は
色と形を変える

洗われた空が
裸の屋根に衣を懸ける

散らばる願望の骨の中から
昼間がその夢を吸い取る

I SEE YOU

through the door

I want my hands in your shirt

in the silver shades
of your hair

when you see me
the sea in our eyes

opens

ドアーの向こうに

　　　私は貴方を見る

両手を入れたい貴方のシャツの中に

銀色に霞むあなたの
　　　　髪の中に

貴方が私を見詰めると
二人の目の中で

　　　　　　海が広がる

WITHOUT NAME
> *or destination*

the clarity of madness
strikes the hour

名前も無く
　　定めも無く

狂気という明確なものが
その時を襲う

I WILL
if I can

reach out
    to be
intoxicated

not by
    you

そうしたい
　もしできるなら

恍惚の世界
　　　に
　飛び込みたい

貴方に酔って
　　　ではなく

FACING GREY LIGHT

through the ashen tree

I am nobody's song

you take root in the mirror
of the earth

I feed the birds your name

灰色の光に向かい

骨灰の木を抜け

私は誰の歌でも無い

貴方は大地という鏡に
根ざしている

私は貴方の名前を小鳥たちに食べさせる

CAUGHT IN A SENTENCE

unable to retain
the lightness of feather

confusion claws
at the meaning
        of word

文章の中にとらえられ

羽毛の軽さを
取り戻せず

困惑が単語の
意味に爪を
　　　　　たてる

WATCHING
> *the distance*

I burn
the colour of Autumn

その隔たりを
　　　見詰め

私は秋色に
燃える

CURTAINS HIDE

the spilled ink
of yesterday's quarrels

the stained bed-spread
the scattered books
   on the unmade bed

so many things
turn the fan of thoughts

カーテンが隠すのは

　　　　こぼれたインクのような
昨日のいさかい

シミのついたベッドカバー
整えてないベッドに
　　　　散らばる数冊の本

いろんなものが
いろんな想いの風を回す

WHEN I REMEMBER
your touch

*a current of gold
melts skin into sun*

貴方の感触を
　　　思い出すと

黄金色の奔流が
肌を太陽に溶かしこむ

YOUR HAND
on my breast

stirs up storms
in the honeycomb
of spine

貴方の手が
私の胸に乗る

ハチの巣の背骨に
巻き起こる
　　　暴風

SOMETIMES

I feel
I am in the land
    of the deaf

or is it that
I am mute

listen
in silence

to the sea
within me

ときどき

私は無音の
国に
　　　いる様な気がする

それとも
私が喋れないのか

黙って
聞き耳をたて

私の中の
潮騒を聞く

PURPLE HYDRANGEAS

紫アジサイ

I have tried since to remember that word

but the sound has sunk back into my sleep

DAVID MALOUF

ずっと覚えておこうとしてきたのは
音では無く言葉が眠りの後ろに沈んでいること

デヴィッド・マルゥフ

David Malouf　前出　15頁参照

THE SUN

raises

      sleepy eyes

    to circling flight

and bird song

      scattered

in trees

太陽が

眠たい

　　　　目をもたげ

　　円く飛ぶものを追う

すると小鳥の歌声が

　　　　木立の中に

散らばった

CLOUDS FLOAT
> *with each breath*

the eagles above
the changing sea

merge into distance

吐息ごとに
　　　雲が浮かぶ

大空には鷲
変わり続ける海

彼方で溶け合う

NO LANGUAGE
captures

the flight of changes

that shape
our inner shrines

言葉が
　　　捉えられないのは

飛翔する変貌

私達の心の
聖所のあり様

WATCH THE SIGNS

that pass unnoticed

in the lavender sky

of sleep

where unexpected

shifts

quicksilver

徴を見詰めよ

ラベンダー色した

空の眠りの中で

　　　　　　フッと

消えていく

　　　　　水銀の

予想外の変貌

DAYS GRAZE
knowing nothing

my skin
 the illusion
of some strange necessity

pulls at the seams
of rose covered pores

 breathing bone

lung branches heave

my hair blooms
purple hydrangeas

日々が草を食む
　　　何も気付かぬまま

私の肌は
　　　何か奇妙な
必然性という幻想

薔薇で覆われた気孔の
縫い目を引っ張る

　　　　骨は息づき

肺の隅々が膨らみ

髪は咲き乱れる
紫アジサイ

HANGING GERANIUMS
in cloud

drink up the murmur of earth
in arched dawn

垂れ下がるゼラニウムは
　　雲の形

曙のアーチの下で
大地の囁きを飲み干している

FROM TRAIN

*landslide of trees
separate concrete blocks*

*blowing TV antennas
in the sky*

列車から

森が地滑りを起こして
コンクリートのブロックを粉砕し

空中では
ＴＶのアンテナを吹き飛ばす

ONE DAY

when I was no
    longer alive

I touched
on the secret of living

and glimpsed
hands knitting

a cloak
of non-being

ある日

私はもはや
　　　　生きていなかったのだが

生きていることの神秘に
触れた

すると二つの手が
非在者の上着を

編んでいるのが
見えた

THEY TOOK AWAY THE BIRDS

and left the sun
on the ground

the wings like broken fists
murmur of flight

the flicker of feather
in the sun's aviary
of transparent shrieks

彼らは小鳥たちを
　　　　攫っていった

太陽は大地に
残されていた

ばらされた拳のような翼は
飛翔を呟いている

羽毛のきらめきは
太陽の鳥小屋で
透明な悲鳴となる

DAYS FALL
through slits in the sky

*sun drops liquid amber
into the parched mouth
of earth*

日々がこぼれる
空のほころびを通して

太陽は干上がった
大地の唇に琥珀の水を
　　　垂らす

WORD SHADOWS
pass into fear

*where sounds flow
dream currents*

and chant an unborn language

言葉の影が
　　　恐怖の中に忍び込む

そこでは音が溢れ
夢の調べとなって

未生の詞を歌う

FROM MY MIND
grows a plant

    or a planet

I dress in moss
emerge moist

and wait
for the meeting

of two continents

私の心から
生まれるのは

　　　草か星か

私は苔をまとい
霧を吐き出し

二つの大陸が
出会う時を

待ち受ける

SPACES OF SILENCE

沈黙の空白

YOUR VOICE

is the call

of the bird

hearing it

I knew

貴方の声は

小鳥の

　　　呼び声

聞けば私には

　　　判るの

flock of crows

white sand in my hair

flame tree

blinding

カラスの群れ

　私の髪の白い砂

　　　　　　　　　　　　炎の木立

　　　　　　　　　　　目がつぶれる

SHIMMERING

*in the folds
of your skin*

*I stab your darkness
    to light*

*and turn you
to gold*

貴方の肌の

襞の中で
ゆらめきながら

私は貴方の闇を刺して
　　　光へ変え

貴方を黄金に
変える

YOU CIRCLE
my pattern of sleeping

and knead me
in the rise
    of morning

we drift
with linen sails

in our river of skin

貴方は私の
眠る姿を丸くなぞり

朝日の
昇る中で
　　　私を揺り起こす

私達は漂う
亜麻色の帆を張って

肌は私達の河

A HUNDRED CANDLES
sprang up in sleep
and lit your flesh

I watch
your melting form

百本のロウソクが
眠りの中で跳ね
貴方の身体に火をともす

私は見詰める
溶けてゆく貴方の身体

YOU FEED ON MY BEING
and warm on my skin

that clothes you
in waking and sleep

貴方は私の存在を食べ
私の肌の上で温もる

私の肌は貴方の衣
眠りの時も目覚める時も

YOU WAKE ME
with breath

warming my body

and move me

to a space

where silences
receive the sun

貴方は吐息で
　　　私を目覚ませ

私の体を温めて

私を空の彼方へ

連れてゆく

そこは静寂が
太陽を受け止める処

MY ARMS
are branches
 of the tree

that is you
within me

私の腕は
木の
　　　小枝

私の中には
貴方が居る

FORGET-ME-NOT

a speck of blue

opens the sky

勿忘草は

一滴の青

大空を開いている

SUNFLOWER

The last petal
*　　　clings*

to its black sun

we hold
*　　　the breath*

of the moment

ヒマワリ

最後の花弁が
　　　　黒い

太陽にまつわる

私達は
　　　息をのんで

その瞬間を待つ

FOREST BONES

骨の林

If the world has
A past - there lived
People of bone

SIGITAS GEDA

もし世界に過去があるなら

過去 — そこには

骨の人々が住んでいた

シギタス・ゲダ

SIGITAS GEDA
リトアニアの詩人・作家（1943 - 2008）

HIEROGLYPHS
of free shadows

over
the vacant face

象形文字は
自由な影

　　　無表情の
顔を覆う

AMBER WASHED
to the shore

sparkle
of underground tree

琥珀は洗われて
岸辺に

地底の
樹のきらめき

琥珀はリトアニアの特産物

BY THE LAKE
I pick clover

listen to legends
of earth as I reach

for green sky

湖の畔で
私はクローバを摘む

緑の蒼穹に
手を差し伸べると

大地の物語が聞こえる

THE TREMBLING BIRCH

betrayed
the quiet of the afternoon

震える白樺は

午後の
静寂を裏切る

FOREST BONES

scratch

the shadows
of my skin

骨の森が
　　　私の肌を

引っ掻いて
様々な影を刻む

LYING IN THE GRASS
I listen
to the whispers of night

the moon lights
my body

くさむらに寝転ぶと
　　　いろいろな
夜の囁きが聞こえる

お月さまに照らされる
　　　私の身体

I BROKE

rye bread

and put home-made cheese
into a linen cloth

tied it with flowers

and sent it
with birds

to my vast
Southern land

ライムギのパンを

千切り

自家製のチーズを
亜麻布にくるみ

花を幾つか結んで

小鳥に託し
広々とした

私の南の
土地へ送った

LISTENING

to the river's flow
in the glow-worm light

I exchanged
the Southern Cross

for the Great Bear

蛍火の中で
小川のせせらぎに
耳を傾けていると

南十字星が
おおくま座に

　　変身していた

THE VILLAGE DOG
licks acid sweat

the blind owl
watches

    the darkening cloud

村の犬が
酸っぱい汗を舐めている

眼闇フクロウが
見詰めるのは

　　暮れなずむ雲

I WATCH

the burnt fields
of Lithuania

as though I were
Australian soil

how will I find
my way home

私が見詰めるのは

リトアニアの
燃やされた田園

オーストラリアは
母国の様だけど

どうすれば
帰途が見つかるか

No more words. In the name of this place
we drink in with our breathing, stay quiet like
a flower, so the nightbirds will start singing

JELALUDDIN RUMI

もう言葉は要らない　この土地の名にかけて
呼吸と共に呑みこみ　花のように
静まろう　夜の鳥たちが歌ってくれるように

　　　　　　　　　　　　　　　ジェラルディン・ルミ

JELALUDDIN RUMI
ペルシャの神秘主義詩人・イスラーム神学の重鎮（1207-1273）

Lidija ŠIMKUTĖ born in 1942 in a small village in Samogitia, Lithuania. Fled Lithuania with her parents during WWII. Spent her early childhood in displaced persons camps in Germany. Arrived in Australia 1949. A dietitian / nutritionist by profession. Studied Lithuanian language and literature by correspondence through Lithuanian Language Institute in Chicago (1973-78) and at Vilnius University (1977, 1987). Traveled widely. Writes in Lithuanian and English with publications in many journals and anthologies. Her poems have been translated into other languages. She has translated Australian poets / writers and other works from English into Lithuanian. She has published 3 books of poetry in Lithuanian: *The Second Longing*, 1978; *Anchors of Memory*, 1982 (both: AM&M Publications, USA); *Wind and Roots*, 1991 (Vaga , Lithuania) .Bilingual collections awaiting publication.

Šimkutė has given readings in Lithuania, Australia, Europe, USA and on radio, TV, and has participated in a number of International Poetry Festivals.

She has received poetry grants from Australia Council and SA Dept for the Arts.

リジア・シュムクーテは1942年リトアニアのサモギチアに在る小さな村に生まれた。第二次大戦中両親と共にリトアニアを離れ、幼少期をドイツの難民キャンプで過ごす。1949年にオーストラリアにのがれ、食事療養士・栄養士として働く。1973－78シカゴのリトアニア言語学院でリトアニアの言語・文学の通信教育を受ける。1977年と1987にはヴィルニウス大学で学ぶ。広く各地を旅する。

おおくの新聞雑誌・作品集に英語・リトアニア語で作品を発表している彼女の詩は多くの国語に翻訳されている。またオーストラリアの詩人や作家の作品をリトアニア語に翻訳している。リトアニア語の詩集は三冊出版されている。「二つ目の願い」(1978)『記憶という碇』(1982) AM& M出版／USA、『風と根っ子』(1991) リトアニア Vaga 社から出版。バイリンガル詩集が数冊出版予定。

シュムクーテはリトアニア・オーストラリア・ヨーロッパ・アメリカで詩を朗読し、ラジオやＴＶでも詩の朗読を放送している。数多くの国際詩祭に参加してきた。

彼女はオーストラリア議会や南オーストラリア文芸局等から様々な助成金を受けている。

Kōichi Yakushigawa b. 1929 in Kyoto. Poet, translator (incl Phillip Larkin, Seamus Heaney & others, including Lidija Šimkutė's four poetry books,) photographer, professor emeritus. Previous editor of "Ravine" literary journal. On the Board of directors, Kansai Poetry Society. Taught English and literature at Doshisha University. Kyoto. Retired 2004. On the Board of Directors of International Byron Society. President emeritus of the Japanese Byron Society.

Awards: The Kyoto City Art and Culture Association Prize 1997, The Order of the Sacred Treasure, Gold Rays with Neck Ribbon 2010, Translator's Special Prize from Japan Translators Society 2014.

Books published:
Poems; "Cityscape with an old dog" and others
Poems & Photos; Talking with Stone Buddha" and others
Academic; "A Study on the British Romantic Poets and Their Social Background" "Reading the Seamus Heaney's World" and others.

薬師川 虹一
1929年京都に生まれる。詩人、随筆家、写真家、翻訳者（フィリップ・ラーキン、シェイマス・ヒーニー、テッド・ヒューズ、リジア・シュムクーテ等）、英文学者（イギリス・ロマン派詩人の研究）、同志社大学名誉教授、詩誌「RAVINE」前編集同人。日本詩人クラブ名誉会員。日本バイロン協会名誉会長。国際バイロン協会前理事。

受賞歴：京都芸術文化協会賞
　　　　日本翻訳家協会特別賞
　　　　瑞宝中綬章

出版書：詩集『疲れた犬のいる風景』他
　　　　詩と写真集『石仏と語る』他
　　　　研究書『イギリスロマン派の研究』他

CONTENTS

Translator's Preface... (8

SILK OF THE SPIDER

INSIDE THE WEB... (20
UNLESS WE DREAM... (22
YOUR VOICE... (24
MY BIRD... (26
YOU MOVE... (28
I'M AFRAID... (30
ACROSS DISTANCES... (32
THE SNAKE RETURNS... (34
BY THE WINDOW... (36
ON WINGS OF BREATH... (38

THE SEA IN OUR EYES

THE CITY'S EYES... (42
I SEE YOU... (44
WITHOUT NAME... (46
I WILL... (48
FACING GREY LIGHT... (50
CAUGHT IN A SENTENCE... (52
WATCHING... (54
CURTAINS HIDE... (56
WHEN I REMEMBER... (58
YOUR HAND... (60
SOMETIMES... (62

目次

訳者序文 ... (9

蜘蛛の糸

紡がれるクモの巣 ... (21
もしお互いの ... (23
あなたの声が ... (25
私の小鳥が ... (27
あなたは動く ... (29
私は怖い ... (31
遠く離れていても ... (33
蛇は戻ってくる ... (35
窓の傍で ... (37
寝息の羽に乗って ... (39

海 は 二 人 の 目 の 中 に

都会の目は ... (43
ドアーの向こうに ... (45
名前も無く ... (47
そうしたい ... (49
灰色の光に向かい ... (51
文章の中にとらえられ ... (53
その隔たりを ... (55
カーテンが隠すのは ... (57
貴方の感触を ... (59
貴方の手が ... (61
ときどき ... (63

PURPLE HYDRANGEAS

THE SUN...   (68
CLOUDS FLOAT...   (70
NO LANGUAGE...   (72
WATCH THE SIGNS...   (74
DAYS GRAZE...   (76
HANGING GERANIUMS...   (78
FROM TRAIN...   (80
ONE DAY...   (82
THEY TOOK AWAY THE BIRDS...   (84
DAYS FALL...   (86
WORD SHADOWS...   (88
FROM MY MIND...   (90

SPACES OF SILENCE

YOUR VOICE...   (94
flock of crows...   (96
SHIMMERING...   (98
YOU CIRCLE...   (100
A HUNDRED CANDLES...   (102
YOU FEED ON MY BEING...   (104
YOU WAKE ME...   (106
MY ARMS...   (108
FORGET-ME-NOT...   (110
SUNFLOWER...   (112

紫アジサイ

太陽が... (69
吐息ごとに... (71
言葉が... (73
徴を見詰めよ... (75
日々が草を食む... (77
垂れ下がるゼラニウムは... (79
列車から... (81
ある日... (83
彼らは小鳥たちを攫っていった... (85
日々がこぼれる... (87
言葉の影が... (89
私の心から... (91

沈黙の空白

貴方の声は... (95
カラスの群れ... (97
貴方の肌の... (99
貴方は私の... (101
百本のロウソクが... (103
貴方は私の存在を食べ... (105
貴方は吐息で... (107
私の腕は... (109
勿忘草は... (111
ヒマワリ... (113

FOREST BONES

HIEROGLYPHS... (118
AMBER WASHED... (120
BY THE LAKE... (122
THE TREMBLING BIRCH... (124
FOREST BONES... (126
LYING IN THE GRASS... (128
I BROKE... (130
LISTENING... (132
THE VILLAGE DOG... (134
I WATCH... (136

About the author... (140
Translator's Postscript... (142

骨 の 林

　　象形文字は ... (119
　　琥珀は洗われて ... (121
　　湖の畔で ... (123
　　震える白樺は ... (125
　　骨の森が ... (127
　　くさむらに寝転ぶと ... (129
　　ライムギのパンを ... (131
　　蛍火の中で ... (133
　　村の犬が ... (135
　　私が見詰めるのは ... (137

　　著者略歴 ... (141
　　訳者紹介 ... (143

Šimkutė, Lidija
Ši 69
Tylos erdvės/Spaces of Silence/Lidija Šimkutė; [iliustracijos
Viačeslavo Jevdokimovo-Karmalitos] – Vilnius: Lietuvos
rašytojų s-gos leidykla, 1999. – 141 p.: portr. Kn. taip pat:
Apie autorę: p. 134
ISBN-9986-39-108-3
*Nauja Australijoje gyvenančios poetės knyga.
Ji rašo lietuviškai ir angliškai, tad čia spausdinamos abi lyrinių
miniatiūrų versijos. Eilėraščiai taupūs, siekiantys paprastumo
ir tikslumo. Išgyvenimai sukuria erdvę, kurioje būsenos ir
žodžiai apie pasaulį prabyla savitai ir mįslingai.*
UDK 888.2 (94)-1

Lidija Šimkutė
TYLOS ERDVĖS / SPACES OF SILENCE
Eilėraščiai / poems

Lietuviškų tekstų redaktorė S. Lygutaitė-Bucevičienė
Angliškų tekstų redakcija ir korektūra – autorės
Leidyklos redaktorius V. Sventickas
Iliustravo V. Jevdokimovas-Karmalita
Knygos dailininkas R. Orantas
Korektorė D. Tunkevičienė
Maketavo D. Kavaliūnaitė

1999 03 08. 0,9 leid. apsk. l. Tir. 800 egz. Užsakymas 417. 248-oji
leidyklos knyga. Lietuvos rašytojų s-gos leidykla, K. Sirvydo 6,
2600 Vilnius, Lietuva/Lithuania.
Spausdino AB „Vilspa" Viršuliškių skg. 80, 2600 Vilnius.
Kaina sutartinė.

詩集　沈黙の空白

2019年10月20日　第1刷発行
著　者　リジア・シュムクーテ
翻訳者　薬師川虹一
発行人　左子真由美
発行所　㈱竹林館
〒530-0044　大阪市北区東天満2-9-4　千代田ビル東館7階FG
Tel 06-4801-6111　Fax 06-4801-6112
郵便振替 00980-9-44593　URL http://www.chikurinkan.co.jp
印刷・製本　モリモト印刷株式会社
〒162-0813　東京都新宿区東五軒町3-19
© Lidija Šimkutė
© Kōichi Yakushigawa　2019 Printed in Japan
ISBN978-4-86000-419-4　C0098
定価はカバーに表示しています。落丁・乱丁はお取り替えいたします。

SPACES of SILENCE / poems

Lidija Šimkutė
English-Japanese bilingual edition
Translation: Kōichi Yakushigawa
First published by CHIKURINKAN Oct. 2019
2-9-4-7FG, Higashitenma, Kita-ku, Osaka, Japan
http://www.chikurinkan.co.jp
Printed by MORIMOTO PRINT CO.,Ltd. Tokyo, Japan
All rights reserved